W9-DAB-950

The
Magic Beans

DEAR CAREGIVER,

The books in this Beginning-to-Read collection may look somewhat familiar in that the original versions could have been a part of your own early reading experiences. These carefully written texts feature common sight words to provide your child multiple exposures to the words appearing most frequently in written text. These new versions have been updated and the engaging illustrations are highly appealing to a contemporary audience of young readers.

Begin by reading the story to your child, followed by letting him or her read familiar words and soon your child will be able to read the story independently. At each step of the way, be sure to praise your reader's efforts to build his or her confidence as an independent reader. Discuss the pictures and encourage your child to make connections between the story and his or her own life. At the end of the story, you will find reading activities and a word list that will help your child practice and strengthen beginning reading skills. These activities, along with the comprehension questions are aligned to current standards, so reading efforts at home will directly support the instructional goals in the classroom.

Above all, the most important part of the reading experience is to have fun and enjoy it!

Shannon Cannon

Shannon Cannon,
Literacy Consultant

Norwood House Press • www.norwoodhousepress.com
Beginning-to-Read™ is a registered trademark of Norwood House Press.
Illustration and cover design copyright ©2017 by Norwood House Press. All Rights Reserved.

Authorized adapted reprint from the U.S. English language edition, entitled The Magic Beans by Margaret Hillert. Copyright © 2017 Pearson Education, Inc. or its affiliates. Reprinted with permission. All rights reserved. Pearson and The Magic Beans are trademarks, in the US and/or other countries, of Pearson Education, Inc. or its affiliates. This publication is protected by copyright, and prior permission to re-use in any way in any format is required by both Norwood House Press and Pearson Education. This book is authorized in the United States for use in schools and public libraries.

Designer: Lindaanne Donohoe
Editorial Production: Lisa Walsh

LIBRARY OF CONGRESS CATALOGING-IN-PUBLICATION DATA
Names: Hillert, Margaret, author. | Jāmānā, Pharidā, 1953- illustrator.
Title: The magic beans / by Margaret Hillert ; illustrated by Farida Zaman.
Description: Chicago, IL : Norwood House Press, 2016. | Series: A
  Beginning-to-read book | Summary: "An easy format retelling of the classic
  fairy tale, Jack and the Beanstalk and his trip up and down the stalk.
  Original edition revised with new illustrations. Includes reading
  activities and a word list"-- Provided by publisher.
Identifiers: LCCN 2015047812 (print) | LCCN 2016009559 (ebook) | ISBN
  9781599537849 (library edition : alk. paper) | ISBN 9781603579254 (eBook)
Subjects: | CYAC: Fairy tales. | Folklore--England.
Classification: LCC PZ8.H5425 Mad 2016 (print) | LCC PZ8.H5425 (ebook) | DDC
  398.2--dc23
LC record available at http://lccn.loc.gov/2015047812

288N—072016
Manufactured in the United States of America in North Mankato, Minnesota.

Margaret Hillert's

The Magic Beans

A Beginning-to-Read Book

Illustrated by Farida Zaman
retold story of Jack and the Beanstalk

NORWOOD HOUSE PRESS

Oh, look.
Here is something funny.
One is red.
One is blue.
One is yellow.

One little one.
Two little ones.
Three little ones.
Look, look, look.

Go down here.
Go down in here, little ones.

Oh, oh.
Look and see.
Here is something little.
Up it comes.

Oh, my. Oh, my.
It is big, big, big.

I can go up.
See me go up.
Up, up, up and away.

Look here, look here.
I see a house.
It is a big, big house.

I want to go in.
In I go.
Jump, jump, jump.

It is big in here.
It is big for little me.

Here is something.
It is not big.
It is little and red.

Look, look.
It can work.
It can make something.

Come to me.
Come to me.
I want you.
Come to my house.
Away we go.

Oh, look here.
Here is something for Mother.
Something for my mother.

And here is something.
We can play it.
We can make it play.
It is fun to play.

Come, come.
Come to my house.
Come to my mother.

Here we go.
Away, away, away.

Oh, my.
Here comes something.
Something big.
Where can I go?

Help, help.
Here I go.
Run, run, run.

And here I go.
Down, down, down.
Mother, Mother.
Here I come.
Help me. Help me.

We can work.
We can make it come down.

Here, Mother.
Here is something for you.

Foundational Skills

In addition to reading the numerous high-frequency words in the text, this book also supports the development of foundational skills.

Phonological Awareness: The /b/ sound

Oddity Task: Say the /**b**/ sound for your child (be careful not to say buh). Say the following words aloud. Ask your child to say the words that do not end with the /**b**/ sound in the following word groups:

tab, tap, tub	ball, bat, cab	cub, job, bus	bean, crib, bib
sob, cub, big	crab, bad, grab	bump, sob, knob	scrub, bun, club

Phonics: The letter Bb

1. Demonstrate how to form the letters **B** and **b** for your child.
2. Have your child practice writing **B** and **b** at least three times each.
3. Ask your child to point to the words in the book that begin with the letter **b**.
4. Write down the following words and ask your child to circle the letter **b** in each word:

barn	boot	lab	cab	bubble	bed	bib
bag	nibble	bone	crumble	bean	dab	thimble

Fluency: Echo Reading

1. Reread the story to your child at least two more times while your child tracks the print by running a finger under the words as they are read. Ask your child to read the words he or she knows with you.
2. Reread the story, stopping after each sentence or page to allow your child to read (echo) what you have read. Repeat echo reading and let your child take the lead.

Language

The concepts, illustrations, and text in this book help children develop language both explicitly and implicitly.

Vocabulary: Opposites

1. The story features the concepts of big and little. Discuss opposites and ask your child name the opposites of the following:

hot (cold)	near (far)	short (tall)
soft (hard)	front (back)	happy (sad)

2. Write each of the words on separate pieces of paper. Mix the words up and ask your child to put the opposite pairs back together.

Reading Literature and Informational Text

To support comprehension, ask your child the following questions. The answers either come directly from the text or require inferences and discussion.

Key Ideas and Detail

- Ask your child to retell the sequence of events in the story.
- What things did the boy find in the castle at the top of the beanstalk?

Craft and Structure

- Is this a book that tells a story or one that gives information?
  How do you know?
- How do you think the boy felt when he was climbing down the beanstalk?
  Why?

Integration of Knowledge and Ideas

- The boy in the story had magic beans. Name the kind of beans you can eat.
- What was the egg made of under the goose?

WORD LIST

The Magic Beans uses the 44 words listed below.

This list can be used to practice reading the words that appear in the text. You may wish to write the words on index cards and use them to help your child build automatic word recognition. Regular practice with these words will enhance your child's fluency in reading connected text.

a	go	make	see
and		me	something
away	help	Mother	
	here	my	three
big	house		to
blue		not	two
	I		
can	in	oh	up
come(s)	is	one(s)	
	it		want
down		play	we
	jump		where
for		red	work
fun	little	run	
funny	look		yellow
			you

ABOUT THE AUTHOR Margaret Hillert has helped millions of children all over the world learn to read independently. She was a first grade teacher for 34 years and during that time started writing books that her students could both gain confidence in reading and enjoy. She wrote well over 100 books for children just learning to read. As a child, she enjoyed writing poetry and continued her poetic writings as an adult for both children and adults.

Photograph by Glenna Washburn

ABOUT THE ILLUSTRATOR Farida Zaman is an Illustrator of many children's picture books and educational material. She has worked for publishers in the UK, USA and Canada. Her global background has given her an insight into different cultures which she applies to her illustrative work. Farida has won many awards in Europe and North America. She lives with her husband, daughter and son in Toronto. www.faridazaman.com